# SILENT NIGHT

By J.E. Taylor

Silent Night © 2023 J.E. Taylor



Cover Art by Adrijana Cernic

# SILENT NIGHT

Everyone thinks the Kringles only work in toy making. Nope. I slay monsters.

But when Christmas rolls around, I protect Santa's sleigh.

So, technically, on Christmas Eve, I'm his little helper.

Most of the time, we deal with a stray rogue monster or two on Christmas Eve. But this year is different. It seems the monsters have decided they want to play with Santa's reindeer and ring his bells.

If I don't put a stop to this madness, not only will Santa be their next meal, but children all over the world will wake to a Christmas that never was.

Not on my watch...

# SILENT NIGHT
# CHAPTER 1

"SANTA CLAUSE IS coming to Town" blares from the phone in my back pocket.

*Ugh. He has the worst possible timing.*

I reach to answer it in the midst of going toe-to-toe with this monstrosity of a monster. The hairy bastard attacked me before I could step through the portal to home hidden at the end of this row of pristinely manicured hedges. It's as if he had been waiting for me behind the shrubs on this deserted street in the west end of New York City. My focus only shifts for a second, but it's enough to give the creature an opening.

Unfortunately, my poor phone goes flying in the air, with the voice of my father yelling, "Chrissy!"

I'm too preoccupied fending off the swipes of his claws with one of the daggers from my belt to attempt to answer my father. Or even begin to bother with the fact that I'll likely have to replace the screen yet again as I hear the thud of my phone coming face-to-face with the cold pavement.

We slowly circle, and I get a good look at this particular being when we pass under a streetlamp. He's hideous. Even more so than the Abominable Snowman. Hairy like a Bergamasco caught in a windstorm, with arched claws that could cut through flesh and bone like butter. And the thing stinks as if he just climbed out of a sewage plant.

All things considered, I would rather be with my father right now, enjoying a mug of hot chocolate and Elise's special Christmas cookies.

My father continues to call my name, his voice growing more desperate by the minute. I'm already late, and this little encounter isn't helping. The monster must sense my impatience because he lashes out.

I jump back as one of his hairy claws swings in my direction. But not far enough. His sharp appendage catches my sweater, slicing it nearly in half. Cool air tickles my bare stomach.

"Damn it," I mutter under my breath. Better the fabric than me, but this is one of my mother's favorite holiday sweaters, and now it'll end up in my rag box.

Aggravation blooms inside me, and instead of continuing to rely on my diminutive dagger to deal with this *thing* in a stealthy manner, I'm done playing around. I slide my knives back into their holders wrapped around my waist, then reach for the sword attached to my back while evading more of his deadly slashes.

Joy, my sword, puts Excalibur in the dust. After all, Joy is blessed with Christmas magic. Forged by the elves, my steel can slice through the wickedest of monsters and still hum every Christmas tune known to man when it's unsheathed.

"Joy to the World" rings out around us when I pull her from her scabbard. I grin as I swing my mighty blade. The moment it hits the beast, he explodes in a poof of red, green, and gold glitter, raining down like a ticker tape parade.

I watch as it falls to the ground, and then I return my sword to its sheath.

Silence falls over the night.

I pick up my phone and breathlessly ask, "What, Dad? And before you say anything, yes, I'm aware that I'm late."

# SILENT NIGHT
# CHAPTER 2

I INSPECT MY ruined sweater and sigh. I *cannot* show up at the North Pole on Christmas Eve like this. Resigned to be later than normal, I turn away from the portal and head back to my apartment a few blocks away, muttering under my breath. This year, I had conceded and worn my mother's favorite Christmas sweater under my leather jacket instead of my normal black attire, and this is the result.

A monster attacked me.

In truth, I probably would have attacked me too with the way this sweater tends to—as my mother puts it—glisten.

My parents are going to be even more upset with me than they already are. A few minutes late on Christmas Eve is one thing, but I will be hitting close to an hour or more once I finally get there, and, to top it all off, showing up in something other than the requested "family festive" Christmas sweater.

My little one-room flat in Greenwich Village is as upscale as I can afford. Monster hunting pays a decent wage, but it's rather sporadic compared to steady work, so I have to ration my money. Although I would have liked something more than a studio apartment, I just don't see the need.

If I want wide-open spaces and a grand bedroom, I can visit the North Pole.

I wade through my drawers, and my fingers fall on the black shirt I usually wear. My mother had begged me to wear something a little more festive, particularly the now mangled sweater she got me a few years back that has yet to make an appearance in public, so I resist the urge to just pull on the familiar fabric and continue my search. Most of my wardrobe consists of grays, deep blues, and black. Outside of the festive red and green sweater the monster ruined, there isn't much of a choice.

I fan through my shirts and stop on a red blouse that's similar in fit and fabric to the black. It will have to do because the rest of my choices just lead me back to the black shirt. I pull the light, silky fabric over my head. At least it'll match my father's outfit, even if it is hidden under my leather jacket.

I stop at my tree, adjusting some of the tinsel strands. My eyebrow cocks up. Maybe if I tie a little tinsel on the hilts of my knives, I'll avoid the swarming scrutiny of the elves. I do just that. With my knives dressed in tinsel and the red blouse, I at least appear a tad more festive.

Perhaps this will ease my mother's disappointment.

I let out a laugh, realizing how absolutely ridiculous I sound, even in my own head. If it were up to her, I'd be holly and jolly, settled into the North Pole "penthouse" they so kindly had expanded with the expectation that I would be living there, with them, wasting away my days, making toys and baking cookies. Now, don't get me wrong, I do love Christmas—especially in the North Pole. However, my "toys" make Rudolph's red nose look completely normal. And don't even get me started on the hockey pucks some may call cookies that are the result of my sad baking attempts.

Though, I will say my hot chocolate making skills do come close to my monster slaying abilities. And I am one of the best monster slayers in the world.

Monsters hear my name and instantly shiver with dread. Although, there was that one that sat and laughed at me when I drew Joy and "Dominic the Donkey" began blaring. But he didn't have much to say after he came face-to-face with Joy's magic touch. I agree, it wasn't her best song choice, but it made for an entertaining victory. Then there are some, like the Abominable Snowman, who turn a new leaf when given the choice between annihilation and leaving their evil behind.

Unfortunately, most meet the sharp end of my sword because monsters usually do not change their spots. Or warts. Or whatever.

I shake the thought from my head and lock up my apartment. I am way too late to drag my feet into a daydream.

I jog back to the portal, press my thumb on the side of the bushes to open it, and step through right into a snowdrift that comes to my knees. God, how I love deep snow. Although we get snowstorms in New York City, it's not the same as the silky white snow of the North Pole.

I pull my boots along one at a time and make my way through the confusing maze of snowdrifts buffering the North Pole from the rest of the world. As soon as I step out of the maze, I grin at the sight in front of me: Santa's house, *my home*, and the town surrounding it. The sleigh barn sits to the side of the house, leaving a path wide enough for the sleigh between the two buildings. Beyond our roof towers the toy factory, which stands on the far side of the courtyard placed in the center of the property. The small elf village sits beyond the toy factory, and it winds around in small, looped neighborhoods. From the sky, it looks like a giant, intricate bow.

Even with their neighborhood, all the elves choose the courtyard to congregate in. A courtyard where I had spent many years playing with other elf children and baby reindeers. Warmth coats my soul along with the prickle of Christmas magic as it seeps into my skin.

I cross to the front porch of the house, kicking the snow off my boots. Before I step inside, I take a deep breath, readying myself, and then I cross the threshold. Before I can collapse onto one of the bright chaise lounges in the entryway, elves swarm around me, all chattering about how I'm not wearing the right clothes for a sleigh ride.

We go through this every year. Every year they want me in brighter clothing, and every year I resist.

"Elise wants you to look more festive this year!" one of the elves complains as they tug at my leather coat, as if to try to strip me of my monster slaying armor.

I fend them off gently until my temper flares when they try to remove Joy. *"Enough.* I conceded to wearing red under my leather jacket instead of black this year, just for your benefit. So enough!" I slash my arms to the sides, pushing them all away.

Silence follows my outburst, and then they scatter like ants.

They want to dress me in thick layers of glitter, velvet, and fur. But I'm a Kringle. The cold doesn't bother me in the slightest. Heat, on the other hand, is another story. Ditch me in the Sahara, and I might have a real problem. But on Christmas Eve, on the sleigh, I need to blend in with the night, not be a beacon like my father with his red coat trimmed with white fur. The only thing black on him are his belt and boots.

I tilt my head back and breathe out a sigh at the scent of evergreen and cookies. My gaze lands on my parents coming out onto the upper landing, hand in hand. The way they gaze at each other melts me to the core. Their eyes sparkle, and I hope that someday I will find that same deep, faithful, and true devotion. Love like that is a once in a lifetime miracle.

My mother's gaze shifts to mine, and that sparkle fades. Her eyes fill with nervous energy. She glances at her watch, her eyes crinkling and her lips pressing into a thin line.

We are late, and it shows in every nuance of my mother's face and body.

"It's about time." My father's less than jolly voice drifts down from the upper floor. He's all decked out in his riding suit. The only myth buster from the fable told all over the world is that Santa Claus is not fat. He's as fit as an eighteen-year-old body builder, despite being well over fifteen hundred years old. The layers of the suit just make him appear…rounder.

He releases my mother's free hand and makes his way down the curving staircase. My mother follows him with her clipboard. A few stray hairs have fallen out of her normally immaculate bun.

"What happened this time?" she asks as they descend the stairs together.

I suck in my initial response to her exasperated tone. I am always a few minutes late; it's my biggest flaw. As much as I intend to get to places on time, something always sidetracks me. It's usually that I can't get a cab or the subway is running slow, but this time, it's a little darker of an excuse.

"I would have been here sooner, but I was attacked by a monster on my way to the portal."

That stops my mother midstride. Her eyes widen, and then she hurries down the stairs as if her baby girl might have gotten hurt. Don't get me wrong, I love my mother, but she dotes way too much for my liking. I guess when you suddenly have a child after being married for fifteen hundred years, you have a right to be a tad clingy.

"Are you okay?" She inspects me for any marks.

"I'm fine, Mom." I roll my eyes at my father, and his smirk says it all. *Be patient with her.* Except I've never been patient in my life. "The bastard ruined the sweater you wanted me to wear," I add as I stop her by grabbing her wrists, stilling her hands. "I'm fine, really."

Those stress lines around her mouth soften, and a smile appears. "It's good to see you, but you and your father need to get moving if you hope to deliver all those gifts by sunrise."

We hustle out back where Santa's sleigh sits all packed up and ready to go. The reindeer shuffle in place, waiting, but I notice a couple of them are slightly swaying. I glance at my father, and he has a concerned crease between his eyes as his gaze lands on the same reindeer I'm glancing at.

"Dasher, Dancer!" he calls out.

Both reindeer look at him with cockeyed smiles. Their muzzles drip with frothy cream.

"For heaven's sake, who gave them eggnog?" Santa waves at his lead reindeer as his gaze pierces the elves rushing around the sleigh.

No one answers. They stop for a moment and trade glances with one another, only to shrug before going back to the task of getting us ready to leave.

Santa shakes his head in disgust and glances at me.

"There's no time to change reindeers." My mother glances with disdain at the two drunken beasts.

Rudolph prances over with his nose glowing as bright as the Christmas lights surrounding the village. But his gait is just as unsteady as the lead reindeer, and the same frothy liquid coats his snout.

He hiccups. "I can lead," he slurs, just before tripping and falling face-first in the snow.

We wouldn't get a mile before this drunk deer crashed us into a mountaintop. At least Dasher and Dancer are still on their feet.

"No, Rudolph. You can stay here and make sure the rest of the deer are... safe," Santa says.

Christmas Eve is a prime night for the snow monsters to attack because my dad isn't here to defend our town with his potent magic. Every mile away from the North Pole weakens our defenses. And the monsters are partial to reindeer meat.

None of the other reindeer seem to be wearing an eggnog beard. Hopefully, they are able to keep Dasher and Dancer driving straight.

I glance at the elves, looking for the guilty party, but none of them pay us much attention as they prepare the sled for launch. Something about their lack of concern strikes me, and I look at my mother.

Her eyes are hard as she scans the elves, and I can't help the worry coursing through me. When her gaze meets mine, I give her a nod. She knows I will keep my father safe, and with two drunken reindeer, it might mean being strapped into a sleigh gone wild. Although I do fight monsters for a living, driving an out-of-control sled leaves me antsy.

"Come on, Chrissy. Let's get this show on the road." Dad claps me on the back and leads us to the sleigh. He gives my mother a lingering kiss that makes my cheeks heat to watch, so I look away. "Stay safe," he says, like he always does.

"You, too," she replies. But instead of the usual excitement that goes along with Christmas, there is worry in her eyes that sends a shiver up my spine. She meets my gaze and blows me a kiss.

I catch it in my hand and return one back at her.

My stomach flutters in warning, and every cell in my body vibrates. An uneasy nervousness flushes my skin, and I sense a hard night coming.

# SILENT NIGHT
# CHAPTER 3

TAKEOFF IS A bit rough, but after we rise into the air, the turbulence caused by the wobbling of Dasher and Dancer smooths out. We head to the portal that takes us over the Pacific Ocean near the Christmas Islands, where we always start our travels, and the plan is to move west across the globe.

Usually, we break through the barrier just as the sun is setting, but tonight, darkness has already shrouded the land. A testament to just how late we are and how sluggish the reindeer seem to be tonight.

The first few islands bring about nothing that alarms me, and I find myself relaxing in the seat next to my father as we bound from hut to hut on these tiny remote islands. I cannot help but be amused at the transition from an almost microscopic speck in the night sky, to the fully fledged sleigh as we blast through the time zones.

As we start our descent into Upper Hutt, New Zealand, movement to my right catches my eye. I stare out into the clouds, confused. What looks like a winged reindeer barrels at us at a speed much faster than we're moving.

Dad lands the sleigh on the next roof, but before he can get out with his sack, that flying deer crashes into Blitzen, nearly knocking the entire sleigh off the house. Santa goes flying, and I grab for him, catching the hem of his jacket and hauling him back into the teetering sleigh.

Blitzen barks in pain as the peryton attempts to pull his antlers from the reindeer's shoulder so he can attack yet again. The beast hisses as he pulls, like he's just as spitting mad as I am.

I make sure my father is stable on his feet before I let go of him and reach for Joy. Unsheathing it makes "Jingle Bell Rock" echo off the rooftop. I leap in the air, bringing the point down through the peryton's neck. The sickening snap of its spine is muted by the spontaneous combustion into that red, green, and gold glitter that my sword's typical kill shot makes.

Just as I slide Joy back into her holster, the neighbor's front porch light flips on.

"Shit! Dad, go dark!"

My father presses the only non-festive button on the sleigh, and we become invisible to the human eye. Just in time, too, because the neighbor's door swings open, and a gentleman comes out with his forehead scrunched in confusion. He looks this way and that, searching the darkness for the source of the Christmas music that had just blasted through the neighborhood. He shakes his head and steps back inside his house. With the slam of the front door and the porch light flicking off, we are in the clear.

I wave my father toward the chimney, reminding him of why we're here, and he swipes his finger across his nose before turning into a magical line of sparks that make their way down the chimney.

Christmas magic is both powerful and beautiful at the same time, and tonight is the only night that it is infused in my bones and not just in the steel of my sword. I can wield it into a protective shield through song and form it into anything, as long as I believe.

If my father ever retires, I might inherit the magic he harbors, but that means I would need to retire from monster hunting, and I don't want to do that. No matter how magical this night is, I thrive on the chase as well as ridding the earth of things children and adults alike fear.

Toy making and distribution simply don't give me that same rush.

After my father disappears, I spin toward Blitzen, sheathing my sword and silencing its chirpy melody. I gently stroke my palms across his wounds, pushing my temporary Christmas magic outward and wishing for his injuries to mend.

He whines under my healing touch.

"I know it hurts," I murmur softly in his ear. "But you will be better than before." My hand brushes the last of the cuts, making them disappear as if they were never there.

My father climbs back into the sleigh, and I settle into the seat beside him.

"It has been a very long time since I've seen a peryton." He mushes the reindeer to the next stop as he shakes his head with disbelief. "I thought they were extinct."

"Well, the monster that attacked me in New York hasn't been seen in decades, either," I say as he secures his bag. "I don't even know what the name for that one is, but I can tell you that in all my discussions with other monster hunters, that thing has never been described."

Santa pauses and looks at me before glancing at the sky around us. He nibbles on his bottom lip as if there's something more I should know about, but as soon as that doubt glazes his eyes, it dissipates, and he turns to do his job. "Keep vigilant." He tosses those words over his shoulder at me as if I'm anything but attentive on these Christmas treks.

I nearly laugh, but I'm not sure if that lob was meant for me or the reindeer. Everyone besides Dasher and Dancer are looking out at the night sky, their muscles twitching under their heavy hides as if expecting another attack.

Hell, my muscles are tight, too, and my hands ache to hold Joy. But Dad prefers silence on this night as opposed to filling the eve with music. The less attention drawn to the sky, the more mysterious Christmas morning is for the children.

And this night is all about bringing children the wonder of the season.

# SILENT NIGHT
# CHAPTER 4

IT TAKES US a few more portals going north to south and back before we're over Russia, with Moscow looming in the distance. The clock on the dashboard clicks off the minutes left, and we both stare at it as the seconds slip away. With our lead reindeer still reeling from the eggnog, we are still woefully behind.

At this pace, we'll be hitting Hawaii and Midway when the sky was on the verge of daybreak, which isn't ideal, and it means we'll be late for Mom's Christmas dinner.

Santa mutters under his breath, pulling my eyes to him. I follow his line of sight, and it feels as if an electric zap runs through me. In the distance, more winged creatures dance across the moon. I count at least six beasts before they fade into the night sky beyond the moon's illumination. Even at this distance, I can tell they are large enough to do damage.

"Crap." I jump to my feet and reach for my sword.

"Chrissy!" Dad exclaims before I can unsheathe the music maker. His pained gaze finds mine.

I don't care that he wants silence on our travels. I need to defend this sleigh. I pull Joy from her scabbard, and she belts out "We Wish You a Merry Christmas."

"This is my job for the other three hundred and sixty-three days of the year." I smile at his questioning glare. Turning away, I debate on where I should launch my attack. If I'm too close to Santa, I run the risk of slicing him with Joy. And if I cut deep enough, that will ruin Christmas for the rest of the globe.

But if I'm too far away, he could get attacked. That thought layers a cold chill over my skin.

He cannot be defenseless.

I pull out two daggers and flip them so I'm holding the sharp ends before extending them to my father. "If they come near you, swipe them with these."

He eyes the approaching monsters and takes the weapons without question. Santa may be jolly, but he is no pushover. After all, he was the one who taught me a lot of defensive moves before I left the North Pole.

He made me into the badass I am today.

I shake the thought away and refocus on our current situation. My gaze lands on the white fur lining his red coat. "Hopefully you won't get blood on your fur."

"I'm sure it will be just fine," he retorts, but his eyes betray him.

It's as if he has inside knowledge that I don't. I'll have to have a serious talk with him after these beasts are taken care of.

But for now, whether I can protect the reindeer and Santa at the same time all depends on my positioning. I move to the front of the sleigh, balancing between the polished sleigh and the harness bar that connects all the reindeer.

With a quick glance at the sky, I calculate how long I have before they reach us. Leaving the deer vulnerable could be a problem. Hell, having two drunk deer leading us *is* a problem, but it isn't something I can solve at the moment. Though they should see the ramifications of their little eggnog adventures, I don't want them to be harmed.

I glance at our situation, flying above the dark, deserted ground below us. Something in my brain clicks. The reindeer are exposed on the underside should there be an attack from below.

There is only one way to handle this. I start singing along with Joy, building up my protective magic. It swells inside me. Unfortunately, my ability to direct it is limited, and when I direct it to fly underneath the reindeer, only a portion of the team is covered. Six of the eight reindeer look as if they are running on a golden path that remains steady underneath them. However, the last two, Donner and Blitzen, are still vulnerable.

If some poor, unfortunate monster decides to gut one of the front reindeer, they won't get very far. My protective layer is the equivalent of a kill shot with Joy.

That golden barrier will stay in place for as long as I keep singing.

My father's deep, baritone voice joins mine, and his magic swells, connecting to my protective barrier and extending it underneath the sleigh itself. Of course, Santa's voice is like listening to the angels sing, and the reindeer respond by gliding through the air like a hot knife through my mother's sweet rolls.

Joy transitions to "God Rest Ye Merry Gentlemen." The staccato beat matches my thundering pulse as the winged creatures approach.

The sleigh dips, as if aiming for a landing on another roof.

"We cannot bring these beasts into a human dwelling!" My father breaks his song, leaving the sleigh vulnerable. "Circle higher in the sky until we dispatch these things." He ties off the reins to the controls and bursts back into song, helping fortify the barrier below.

I squint, trying to figure out what they are, but a cloud drifts over the moon, blocking our ability to identify them. However, they are close enough now for me to catch a red reflection where I think their eyes are.

"What are they?" I whisper between verses.

"Gargoyles," Santa hisses as he takes another breath and returns to the melody.

*Gargoyles?*

*What the actual hell?*

That's a beast I've never fought. They are inherent protectors, not mindless attack monkeys. And the ones I've met certainly did not have evil red eyes. Another fact surfaces in my mind, making my eyes widen.

*Gargoyles only attack under command.*

Which means someone is orchestrating these attacks.

I swallow hard and glance back at my father. Who would want to harm Santa Claus?

Who would want to harm *my father?*

The burn of anger starts in my toes and travels up my body into my hands, changing the tune Joy is casting out.

"You're a Mean One, Mr. Grinch" comes sailing out of my mouth as if I'm hurling insults at the gargoyles.

I will find out who led this attack, and I will lay waste to every last one of them.

It's as if the gargoyles sense my mood shifting into full battle mode. They plummet toward us like cannon blasts in the sky. I hold Joy at the ready, and my father has both blades poised in his hands. We continue to sing to protect the reindeer. The magical glow flares around Joy as they attack.

I swing, spin, and dance on the backs of the reindeer as glitter fills the air around us. My father grunts from behind me, and I leap onto the sleigh to fillet the gargoyle that has my father's arm in his mouth.

There is no time to inspect his wounds. A deer screams. I spin back and sprint across the joist between the reindeer, swinging Joy around as if it's a baton. With a thrust, I take out the creature on Dancer's back as the end of the song flows from my mouth.

The tune Joy decides on next is "Do They Know It's Christmas?" and the irony is not lost on me as I strike down another gargoyle.

"Where are they coming from?" I shout between hoarse verses.

When no answer comes from behind me, I turn, and horror fills me at the sight of two gargoyles tearing into my father's coat. I want to launch Joy at them, but it would only serve to harm my father more than he was already hurt. Instead, I run and swing my blade, slicing into the two.

But it isn't a kill shot, and they turn their sights on me. The moment they release my father from their monstrous hands, I cut them down with a battle cry that shakes the night around us.

I can hardly breathe, unable to fully grasp the horror of what they've done to my father. His eyes seem to lose their frantic quality as his gaze finds mine. He offers me a warm smile that soon turns to a grimace as he tries to move.

"Don't," I chide, laying Joy down next to me on the seat. She hums quietly, and I reach to loosen my father's belt so I can see the damage the creatures caused. His suit is all but ruined and underneath, his blood flows at an alarming pace.

"Chrissy," he gasps as the reindeer descend onto a nearby roof, the movement jostling both of us.

I don't think the reindeer understand how dire the situation is. Not with them waiting so patiently for Santa to do his job.

But Santa is not in any condition to spread Christmas cheer.

When his eyes slip closed, my heart plunges into a free fall.

# SILENT NIGHT
# CHAPTER 5

IT'S CHRISTMAS. A time where miracles come true.

I blink back the sudden swell of tears blurring my vision and slide Joy into her holder. A deathly silence flows over us, and I rub my hands together, calling on every last ounce of my Christmas magic.

I need more than just the spirit of Christmas to bring my father back from the brink. I need a miracle from God above.

I close my eyes, press my hands against Santa's shredded skin, and let "Silent Night" fall from my lips. I put my entire soul into the song and push all my healing Christmas magic into him.

The reindeer's voices join in with me, singing. The noise drifts into the night sky like a glorious prayer. Lights all over the neighborhood we're in start snapping on, creating a soft glow on the street below us. When warmth flows through me, I glance to the light radiating from the heavens above. My hands tingle with the power of the Lord as it flows into my father's form, mending the cuts and stanching the outflow of blood.

As the final note drifts on the air, Santa inhales sharply, as if waking from a nightmare. His gaze jumps to mine and then down at my hands splayed out on his chest before snapping back up in wide surprise.

"You…brought me back?" he asks.

Exhaustion ripples through me, but I can't help but smile down at him and nod. I lean back on my haunches and pull my blood-covered hands away from him, wiping them on my thighs. "Christmas magic," I whisper, acutely aware of the curious voices on the street below.

He grabs my hands and squeezes them as he sits up and looks around. Before I know it, he releases me and turns into that familiar stream of sparkles, going from chimney to chimney despite the onlookers below.

He comes back a few minutes later with a bag that is significantly lighter than before. He just smiles, unties the reins, and snaps them.

We are off once again. The rest of the Eastern Hemisphere goes without another attack, and it isn't until we're over the Atlantic Ocean that I feel the knot between my shoulders unwind for a moment.

"I've never been able to heal wounds with Christmas magic," Santa says softly. "Maybe produce a bandage out of thin air, but you mended my skin like their claws never tore through it." His voice is low, as if speaking of the deed will undo what I did.

"I healed Blitzen too." I wave toward the last reindeer in the pack.

"I don't know if you noticed, but we're back on track, as well. Whatever you did electrified all of us." Dad slides his gaze to me, and the reindeer nod in unison.

I laugh and wave his words away. "Without—"

"Don't brush this away like it isn't something incredibly special," he says in that stern tone of his.

It's almost a reprimand, but I'm old enough to merely roll my eyes.

"I kill monsters for a living, Dad." I can't think of anything else to say, and frankly, it's slightly embarrassing to be called out for a gift you have only one day a year. "Besides, this"—I raise my hands—"is Christmas magic. I only have it while we're delivering gifts to the world's children." I shrug and bring my hands back to my lap, where they wrestle together as I fidget under his stark gaze.

"How did you do it?"

I press my lips together as I consider the question. When I stroked Blitzen and wiped his wounds away, I simply believed I was able to heal him with that touch because of the Christmas magic swelling inside me. Same with my father.

As lights of another city dance in the distance, I glance at him. "You taught me Christmas is a time of miracles, and I believed."

# SILENT NIGHT
# CHAPTER 6

I ALWASYS FIND the South American landscape to be awe-inspiring. The thick jungle alongside the mountains rivals the Alaskan countryside and even that of the North Pole, in my opinion.

And the islands in the Caribbean all decked out in Christmas cheer are charming without seeming cheesy. My grin seems to be a constant staple as we island-hop our way to the southern tip of Florida in the United States.

This year, we decide to do a zigzag from south to north and east to west, so we can take advantage of the time differences in order to get home before my mother's meal is ruined. Since I healed my father, he seems to be fueled by something, making him unnaturally faster, and we have more than made up for the initial slowness as well as the time we lost during the monster attacks in the Eastern Hemisphere.

Thankfully, outside of the initial attack in New Zealand, the Southern

Hemisphere has been calm. But that changes when we reach the interior of the Northeast near the Canadian border. It's as if an entire herd of perytons were waiting for us to arrive.

It's hard to miss the horde as it approaches due south to our northern heading. My heart rate picks up and I stand, hopping onto the front edge of the sleigh as I unsheathe Joy. She tingles in my hands as "I'll Be Home for Christmas" slashes across the night sky, with both my father's and my voices joining in. When the reindeer start to sing, the magic of Christmas encompasses the reindeer in a cocoon of comfort.

But it leaves Santa and me vulnerable.

"Move forward a little," I say between choruses, jumping onto the seat behind him. He leans into me, pinning me to the back of the sleigh so I can't tumble out, and gives me a grim nod.

His suit is still in tatters from the gargoyle attack, and if the perytons get within range to shish kabab him on their antlers, that could prove to be more devastating than the last attack. The gargoyles had not gotten to his heart, but a well-placed antler could spear right through it.

"What's the plan?" Dad asks, still steering straight for the pack.

"Use the magic surrounding the reindeer. It acts like my sword and if any get through, well, Joy will do the job."

"So, instead of evasive action, we play a little chicken." My father grins and that light that always seems to be in his eyes brightens.

Santa is enjoying the idea of battle, like he used to enjoy our sparring sessions while he taught me the different forms of martial arts. I didn't think I'd live to see the day where we would be in a fight together, but the shine in his smile tells me his adrenaline is running just as high as mine, even without a weapon.

"I'll be Home for Christmas" transitions to "We Need a Little Christmas," and our voices seem to echo off the land.

Dad steers the sleigh straight for the perytons and after the leading ones hit the magical barrier around the reindeer, and turn into a glitter storm, the rest of the perytons scatter like seagulls when a child runs right for them on a beach.

Santa pursues a group that veer to the right as I spin Joy over my head, protecting us from above. But that leaves us vulnerable on both sides. I keep sweeping my gaze back and forth to ensure that an attack is not coming in either direction.

The reindeer sing louder as they dash from peryton to the next peryton, laughing with joy as the beasts explode into glitter when the barrier hits them. I guess it's better than sending torrents of blood over us.

Joy transitions to "Feliz Navidad," and the upbeat tempo seems to give us all an extra boost. I'm swinging away around us, chopping down those that try to attack from the sides, when a sudden sting throws me forward. I nearly lose Joy as I sail over the front of the sleigh.

It takes me a moment to realize my left shoulder is impaled on one of the monster's antlers. Pain flares, and I cry out as it lifts me higher, away from the sleigh. Santa looks up at me with wide eyes. He doesn't see the two perytons aiming at his blind side.

"Bank right!" I call out, and the reindeer do as I say, still singing the song that Joy leads. I cannot see the sleigh below to make sure they turned in time to save my father from the same fate.

I snarl as the peryton takes me higher and farther from Santa. I swing Joy behind me and am rewarded with a puff of glitter. Then gravity takes hold and I'm in a free fall, without the sleigh or reindeer below to catch me. Another peryton charges for me in the sky. The blaze in its eyes makes me swallow hard. His antlers are longer than my sword.

The singing becomes louder, surrounding me like a warm blanket. I don't dare deviate my attention away from the murderous beast charging at me, or look at the drop below that would certainly steal my life away. Magic strokes my skin, reaching for me, pulling me back to safety.

Before the beast reaches me, Dasher comes up beneath me, and I land on his back with a thump that sends air rushing from my lips. And yet again, I almost lose my grip on Joy.

My shoulder screams upon impact, but no sound escapes from my mouth as I try to make my lungs pull air in instead of feeling this vortex sucking my last breath from me. The barrier in front of Dasher and Dancer rams into the peryton who thought he'd target me, turning him into a plume of colorful glitter.

I swing my gaze around, looking for the rest of the monsters, but the sky is empty. It seems we annihilated all of them, or the survivors decided they liked living more than whatever deal they had made to take down Santa.

I wish I had a chance to pry a name from their dirty mouths.

I wish I had a target for this unhealthy anger rising inside me.

"That was the last one," Santa calls to me.

I turn and nod, sliding Joy back into her sheath. Before I climb off Dasher, I stroke his head and neck and give him a hug.

"Thanks for saving my ass," I whisper.

"Thanks for saving all our asses," he says back, glancing over his shoulder. "Lord knows some of us are not worthy." His cheeks turn red, and he faces forward.

"You and Dancer are worthy."

He huffs at me. "We didn't realize that eggnog was spiked," he replies softly. "It was just left outside by the back door for anyone to get into, and it smelled so good."

I blink and look at the two reindeer. "You didn't sneak a drink through the kitchen window to get it?"

They shake their heads. "That is *not* allowed." Only one reindeer would break the rules without so much as a reprimand, and he had been more blitzed than these two. "Besides, Rudolph found it first, and Dancer and I just wanted a taste," Dasher adds. "Tell Santa we're very sorry."

"I will." I pat his neck. "But I think you just made up for it." I climb off him onto the pole connecting all the reindeer to the sleigh. "You didn't happen to see who put the bowl out, did you?"

"No, we didn't," both Dasher and Dancer say at the same time.

Disappointment laces my mouth, overriding the dull throbbing in my shoulder. I head forward, with my gaze dancing around the sky, looking for the next attack. When I glance at my father, his brow furrows with worry.

I step over the front of the sleigh and collapse onto the seat next to him.

"You're injured." His voice holds pain and anguish.

I glance down at my shoulder and try not to wince as I take stock of my torn jacket and the equally damaged skin beneath. At least the monster was kind enough not to hit any bone. It's a clean shot right through me. "It'll heal."

My father hands me the reins, then takes hold of both sides of my body. He closes his eyes, and a deep crease appears as he brings his eyebrows together in concentration. His cheeks turn red, and finally, opens his eyes once more.

"What are you trying to do?" I cock an eyebrow at him.

He drops his hands and stares at his bloody palms as though they failed him in some manner. With a sigh and a wiggle of his fingers, he has two of those bandages with the self-stick edges. "Lean forward," he says, proceeding to patch up the entry and exit wounds.

# SILENT NIGHT
# CHAPTER 7

WE CONTINUE DELIVERING gifts as if it were just another normal Christmas Eve. But tonight has been anything but normal, as evidenced by my father's nearly shredded and blood-stained suit and my torn jacket. Black leather doesn't show blood the way his white fur does, and I stare at the stains as he settles into the seat next to me. My wound itches and I shift in the seat, stanching the overriding need to scratch at it.

"Who would want you dead?" I meet his gaze with my own.

He purses his lips, as if there is a long list to consider, and as he looks out at the reindeer, he sighs and snaps the reins.

It's all a bit unnerving.

"Is there someone?" I press, because his reaction is not what I had expected.

"There could be a few. I got a little ornery with some of the elves the other day when they tried to bring up making my toy factory a union shop.”

I snort a laugh. “Union? Why do they want a union?”

“Fair wages, reasonable hours, ability to move up in the ranks. That’s what they spouted.” He sighs and wipes his face. “All the normal things a union shop wants to control. And I got the explicit feeling that the last demand was the most important. Even though there is no true upward movement among elves. Sure, they can go from toy making to management, but that’s as high as they can go. Unless they’re vying for my job, but that isn’t possible.”

I chuckle and shake my head. “Union shop at the North Pole. What a farce.”

He glances over at me with a nod. "That was my reaction. And apparently it angered some of the boys."

I am compelled to point out the obvious. "Anger and premeditated murder are two different beasts."

Santa shrugs. "True. But I'd know who, along with the very reason why, if we were being attacked by an actual person. The naughty list would spell it out for me like a neon beacon." He directs the reindeer toward a nearby neighborhood. "Elves and monsters are not on any of my lists." He glances at me again. "And the only beings with enough magic at their disposal to control the monsters reside in or around the North Pole."

"We need to figure out who's behind all this." I scan the horizon. My gaze sweeps back and forth restlessly and my shoulder throbs in time with my heart. "What about the Winter Warlock?"

Santa rolls his eyes. "It isn't a witch or a warlock. They are on my list. I would know if it was one of their kind."

"Yes, but the Winter Warlock *was* evil in the past."

My father sighs. "He was never evil. He was just lonely, and while he did scare people, he never harmed a soul. Besides, he's not the type who would put out a filthy contract on my life. If he wanted me dead, he wouldn't leave it to anyone else to do the deed. He would do it himself."

My father is entirely too trusting. I pinch the bridge of my nose, thinking I don't discount the Winter Warlock as a suspect. He has enough magic to control monsters, after all. "Who were the elves that asked about turning our toy shop into a union shop?"

"Sunny and Vale."

The oldest damn elf in the entire North Pole, along with one of the dumbest. I wipe my face as we land on another roof. Then I give my father a strained smile, and he swirls into action, delivering gifts to the houses around us while I mull over the two names.

Sunny isn't just the oldest, either. He's in charge of the reindeer on

Christmas Eve, as well as the toy factory.

"Did anyone see who left the eggnog out?" I ask, and the exasperation of our situation bleeds through into my voice.

Cupid cocks his head as he turns toward me. "I didn't see who left it out, but I'm pretty sure it was Elise who took the empty eggnog container inside. She didn't look happy about it, either. I caught some of her mutterings about who under the heavens left the eggnog pot outside, of all places."

"Elise?" Elise is Sunny's wife, and she's in charge of the kitchen on most days. She makes a scrumptious Christmas cookie, too. I bite my lower lip as Cupid nods at me. She is not naturally chipper like most elves. She practically glowers at me whenever I come home, whereas the others smile and flit around me, asking a thousand and one questions.

The lights dance back into the seat next to me before they form back into my father.

I tell him, "Cupid says Elise brought the bowl in from outside, but she seemed agitated with it not being in the right place." I tilt my head. "Do you think Sunny could be angry enough that he would manipulate the monsters to try to kill you?"

Santa levels his gaze at me, shaking his head. "You might want to stick with monster slaying. Your sleuth skills seem to be lacking." He snaps the reins, and we are off to the next neighborhood.

"Dad, I thought you said I could do anything if I put my mind to it." I cross my arms and slouch in my spot next to him on the seat. But that doesn't stop me from keeping a sharp eye on all that surrounds us. My nerves tingle, telling me the danger is far from over.

My sideways glance at my father reveals that tic in his jaw that he usually has when he's clenching it. The jolly Santa I'm used to is nowhere to be found. He is just as on edge as I feel.

"You can, but I doubt we'll be able to solve this mystery tonight. Not when I have a job to do and a time limit in which it must be done." He sends his own strained smile my way. "In other words, I can't focus on this until we have a reprieve over the Pacific."

We land effortlessly. And then he is gone in a sprinkle of light.

I run my hand over my face. "God above, give me the strength to keep him safe tonight." I glance at the heavens. My injury saps a little more of my power as the evening wears on.

If we have to battle more gargoyles and perytons, I'm not sure I have the strength to keep them at bay. Not with a bum shoulder that stings every time I shift my weight. Even with Joy and Christmas magic at our disposal. I lean my head back against the hilt of my sword, and it vibrates as if it's trying to tell me all will be well.

I smile and sigh. My sword is even more optimistic than I am. I start to sing the song that inspired me to name my sword.

"Joy to the world, the Lord is come. Let Earth receive her King." The reindeer join in, and the song drifts softly over me. Magic tingles in my fingertips and down my spine as it takes hold of me.

The Christmas spirit is still alive and vibrant, and it fills me with the same emotion as my sword's namesake. I smile at the stars above, and all my doubt is erased away.

I truly believe in the magic of this season.

# SILENT NIGHT
# CHAPTER 8

I T ISN'T UNTIL we are north of Mt. Rainier and heading toward Seattle that another disturbance appears in the distance. On the West Coast, there's more cloud cover than the rest of the country, and it is hard to discern clouds from real threats.

My muscles tense. The tic in my father's tight jaw is back and it seems he stiffens as well. I rise to my feet, ignoring the protest of all my muscles, especially my shoulder, which sings a very loud and obnoxious tune of pain.

I pull Joy from her sleeve.

"Holly Jolly Christmas" rings out around us. I usually join in on this song, but I'm feeling sluggish and the best I can do is whisper the words. However, both the reindeer and my father seem to be all in with the song, sparking magic in the night.

I squint as the clouds move in a strange manner. We are vulnerable here and don't have enough power to wrap the sleigh and the reindeer in our protective buffer. I glance up at the thick cloud cover once more. If we were above this cover, it would be easier to defend the sleigh.

"Go up. Above the clouds."

My father looks at me and then at the approaching mass, then pulls the reins back. The reindeer shoot almost vertically up, and I slam into the seat with the force. Thankfully, I don't tumble right over the back or lose hold of Joy.

As soon as we clear the cloud cover, the moon shines over the layer, making it look silver against the black sky. We continue singing, and the magical barrier stretches out below us.

Something bumps into the sleigh, and a familiar burst happens. In front of us, nearly a half dozen monsters hit the barrier, and they burst into Christmas glitter. I am unsure what these are until one plunges through the clouds to the side of the sleigh.

"Duck!" I yell at Santa before swinging in the direction of the gargoyle that reaches for him. Joy slices through meat and bone, and then the ugly thing turns to glitter.

"Behind you!" he cries to me.

Instead of stopping my swing, I spin, bringing Joy with me.

The gargoyle is closer than the other one. Close enough for its claws to reach me. But I throw my injured arm up in a block, wincing at the drag of claws down my forearm just before the beast meets Joy and bursts into glitter.

I sit down hard, breathing out in heaving pulls as my gaze travels around us to be sure we aren't still under attack. When my gut tells me we're safe, I slide Joy back into her holder and give my father a nod.

He turns the sleigh, plummeting through the clouds to the next roof. Instead of immediately getting out, he conjures another bandage and wraps my arm in silence. His gaze locks on my face, and then he sits back in the seat once he's done.

"This is what you do every day?"

I chuckle and shrug. "I usually don't get impaled on an antler, but yes. This is my job." He's seen me dispatch a monster or two before when we've run across them, but it was rare, and it usually happened in remote areas like the Himalayas or the Andes. "Go. Time is ticking," I say with a nod toward the chimney.

In a blink, he turns into that magic stream of light.

I close my eyes for a moment and then reach down under the dash of the sleigh, where I slipped a bottle of water before we set out. Thankfully, it hadn't been dislodged and lost in all our evasive maneuvers throughout the night. I crack it open and take a sip. The cool liquid slides down my throat like it was heaven-sent. I cap it and stow it back where I found it, relishing the silence of the early hour.

As we go north, we might hit some snow. I smile at the prospect.

A scream shatters the night, and I'm instantly on my feet, scanning the street below. My father stumbles out the front door of the last house he had magically descended into the chimney to deliver his gifts. He makes it as far as the road and then falls to his knees.

"Go!" I shout and the reindeer take off, landing right beside him on the wet asphalt.

I'm out, with Joy in my hands. I don't even look up at my surroundings as both Joy and the reindeer sing in the night. My father's neck is slashed, and he glances at me as if all is lost.

I lay Joy across his chest and put my hands on both sides of his throat. Joy switches to "Silent Night," my particular power song, while I sing along and push all my healing magic into my father. His neck mends as Christmas magic swirls around us. My father's eyes blink closed, and I will him to live, even if it means taking every last ounce of my life force.

Santa is still pale, but his neck shows no sign of the gaping wound it had when he fell in the street. His chest rises and falls in even beats. I look up past the trail of blood, and a small child stands at the door of the house with her hand over her mouth.

I climb to my feet, leaving Joy on my father to protect him while I pull daggers from my sheath. Whoever or whatever hurt my father is in this house, and they need to pay.

"Is Santa...dead?" the child asks, her eyes wide and terrified.

I glance at the open space behind her and shake my head. "No, he's resting." Then I crouch down to her level. If this child hadn't screamed, we would have never known my father was in danger. "Did you see who hurt him?"

Her eyes are almost too wide, and her little form starts shaking as if it's freezing out. She nods. "A m-monster," she whispers as her teeth start chattering.

"Is it still in there?"

Her eyes rise to look at something over my shoulder. That's when my brain registers Joy's music growing close. I turn and see Santa standing behind me, with Joy in his hand.

"Stay with her. I have a monster to slay."

"Are you sure you don't want me to take care of this?" I should be the one to kill the monster, but the anger in my father's eyes gives me pause. When he shakes his head, I add, "See if you can find out who is orchestrating this before you deal the final blow."

He nods, stepping around me and the wide-eyed child shivering in the night.

I wonder where her parents are. "Thank you for alerting us," I say, and her gaze moves from my father to me and my bloody hands.

Her chin quivers. "I wasn't supposed to get out of bed until the morning," she whispers.

I want to run my hand through her hair and give her a hug, but I doubt her parents would appreciate waking up to her having dried blood all over her. Although, from the look of the entryway, there is a trail of blood from their living room to the front stoop. The deep timbre of voices rolls out through the hall, and I strain to try to hear the words. But then glitter bursts into the hallway, landing in the red liquid smearing the floors.

Santa walks out with Joy leaning on his shoulder, still singing her Christmas tunes. He swirls his finger, and a small tornado follows him, cleaning up the mess the monster left behind.

I stand as the glitter and blood join in the cleaning twister, following him out to the porch. He hands me the sword with his lips pressed tightly together. Then he nods and turns his attention to the child.

"Dear Samantha, I am sorry you had to see that unfortunate incident. Your house is monster-free now." He smiles at her and pats her head. "Thank you for the cookies and milk. Now you need to go back to your room and back to sleep so all this seems like a bad dream when you wake up." He turns her and scooches her inside, watching as she heads upstairs. Once she is out of sight, he closes the door and marches past me to the sled. The cleaning swirl follows him, erasing the evidence of his near death.

I slide Joy into my sheath, silencing her as I follow and climb into the far side of the sleigh.

# SILENT NIGHT
# CHAPTER 9

MY FATHER DOESN'T SPEAK but he does accept one of my daggers and slides it into his belt before he finishes delivering gifts throughout the rest of North America. Even the light snow doesn't lift his sour mood.

Thankfully, there are no more attacks on the mainland of North America as we finish up our deliveries through Alaska and head south over the Pacific for Hawaii, Midway, and lastly the Baker Islands.

"Do you know who ordered the hit?" I ask, because that is what this is: a hit on his life. I'm not sure whether the attack on me outside the portal was part of this ungodly plan to kill Santa, but it certainly would have made the monsters successful without me there to defend him.

He gives me a curt nod. "The gargoyle overestimated himself." He huffs a laugh. "Or sorely underestimated you. He said he already sent the success message before that child started screaming. They think the monsters killed me." His gaze slashes to mine, and a smile like nothing I've ever seen appears on his face. It's cold and dangerous. "We have the element of surprise."

A shiver slides down my side as my brain catches up. There is one person he's forgetting. "What about Mom?" My heart picks up at the sudden shift in him and the way he snaps the reins, demanding more speed.

"I have to hope they will not harm her," he says. But now that I've asked the question, worry overshadows the anger on his brow. He takes a breath. "We'll have the reindeer drop us off outside before they land in the courtyard."

"And then what? What's your plan?" I lean toward him, and the reindeers' ears shift to catch the conversation.

He looks at the creatures in front of us. "They will only fly for the true Santa, not the traitor who wishes to take over." His lips cock into an evil grin. "That's when we come in from the house, and you can spread Joy around at will."

I blink at him. "How many?"

"Only one gave the orders, according to the gargoyle. Dark magic animated them and controlled them, and that's how they communicated the failures along the way. It's how they lined up the next attack when one failed. Without the black magic animating them, they would have never dreamed of attacking us. And the peryton? Who the hell knows how they got where they were, but I'm willing to bet black magic played a hand in gathering them, too. If I had been certain the gargoyle wouldn't report back to them, I would have let it live. But I've never trusted the reach of black magic. And with your mom at their mercy, we need that element of surprise." He stares out at the darkness surrounding us and sighs. "I'm not entirely convinced that Sunny is aware of this diabolical plan, either."

My brow furrows as my brain catches up. Sunny and Vale came to him about the union, but it couldn't be Vale. Vale couldn't conjure a bow to finish off the wrappings on a Christmas gift, never mind control an entire population of monsters.

My eyes widen as the only other logical elf rises to the surface. "Elise gave the orders?"

He nods. "I wouldn't eat whatever she has prepared tonight, either. I wouldn't put it past her to plan on poisoning every last one of us to get what she wants. There are going to be a lot of hungry and very angry elves tonight."

As soon as we're finished in the Pacific, Santa races to the portal and we barrel through it, stopping outside the towering drifts. We hop off and watch as the unmanned sleigh swirls up and around the peaks to the North Pole and Santa's courtyard.

Usually, Christmas music echoes off the surrounding mountains upon Dad's arrival, but only quiet lingers. In the distance, I swear I hear sobbing.

I glance over at my father.

"I hope your mother forgives me for this little ruse," he says softly before starting for the snowdrift maze and our home with me at his side.

# SILENT NIGHT
# CHAPTER 10

WE STEP IN THE house together. Me in my ruined leather jacket and Santa in his blood-soaked, shredded suit with the blade still stuck in his belt. He didn't need it for the last leg, but he kept it close just in case. He looks just as badass as I feel as we head toward the side entrance to the courtyard.

We stick to the shadows, and all I can hear is a high-pitched female voice trying to calm the crowd of devastated elves. Mom is on her knees, sobbing by the side of the blood-splashed sleigh for the loss of her husband and daughter.

It tears my insides apart more acutely than any of those monsters could. My father's eyes carry the same hurt. Fury rides through every muscle of mine, making my shoulder pound with my increased heartbeat.

The reindeer shift from foot to foot, looking in our direction before trading glances but they keep quiet, just as they should. Even their eyes carry the hard edge of anger.

Sunny comes out of the back door from the main house into the courtyard, wearing the full Santa garb with his arms extended, as if he owns the place. Yet the elf is only a fraction of my father's height and does not instill the same Christmas spirit as the true Santa, despite his overexuberant "Ho-ho-ho."

He slides into the sleigh as though he's going to drive it back to the garage, but the reindeer don't budge when he prompts them by snapping the reins. His expression falls as he looks at the reins, as if the problem lies in the leather ties in his hands.

The reindeer know he isn't in charge of them. They heard my father talking about Sunny's plans on the sleigh. This elf and his wife were responsible for the near death of their beloved Santa. They send a sneer in Sunny's direction, looking at him with all the animosity I feel.

"Jess will be the new cook," Elise announces, waving to my mother as if it is an honor in itself. "And because Sunny is the oldest elf, older than Santa himself, he and I will take up residence in the main house." She smiles sweetly, as if she hadn't planned all this with her husband. "We will make this place run like a well-oiled clock!"

*As if it didn't already run smoothly.* My fists clench, as do my teeth. Rage coils in my belly, turning into a force of its own.

Sunny snaps the reins again, but the sleigh does not budge. "Move, you filthy bastards!"

I trade a glance with my father. Storm clouds gather in his eyes, and thunder rumbles overhead despite the clear skies.

Sunny glances up, and concern paints his brow. He snaps the reins again, to no avail. The reindeer refuse to budge for the fake Santa.

Dad nods, and we step out of the shadows. I draw Joy from my scabbard, and the chilling tune of "The Little Drummer Boy" slices through the silence.

Gasps fill the area, and the crowd parts.

All I see is red when I stare at the two complicit traitors. Vengeance roars up in my blood, and all I want to do is strike them down. No explanation will appease this immense need for justice.

They are monsters, and it is my job to extinguish the unholy beasts.

Elise's eyes widen and then narrow as she realizes her plans of dominating the North Pole have been thwarted. Her face scrunches in frustrated anger.

"Chris!" my mother's voice rings out with relief, and then she is on her feet.

As she runs by Elise, the little witch shoots out her leg, sending my mother to the ground. Then she grabs my mother by the hair and yanks her back onto her knees. From out of nowhere, a knife appears at Mom's throat. "Strike your father down, and I will let your mother live."

Everyone freezes. The somber song plays on, and I glance at Santa. His eyes fill with pain, and he gives me a nod. He wishes to forfeit his life for hers. That is how strong his love is for my mother.

I shake my head. I cannot strike my father down, even if that is his solution to keeping the love of his life alive.

I don't know what Elise expected, but from the snarl she emits, this was not it. "You all think you're better than us. That you are above the elves. You can't even agree to a union to protect us from dangerous work conditions." Elise waves the knife toward us and then places it back against my mother's throat. "And then you bitch and whine about the food placed on your tables, as if it isn't good enough or varied enough or sweet enough. I want more than just an elf's existence. I want to be respected and revered!"

She's screaming now, and all I can do is stare at the knife scraping up and down Mom's throat, leaving a red mark like a rug burn on her skin. The knife hasn't broken the skin yet, but my gut tells me it's only a matter of time.

"I want to be waited on and pampered. I want what you have. Strike him down so I can have the power I crave!" The pitch of her screech echoes off the buildings surrounding us.

I look at my father and know I shouldn't say it, but it rolls out of my mouth before I can stop it. "She's an angry elf."

Santa smirks and nods despite the dangerous tension filling the air.

"That's it." Elise stomps her foot like an irate two-year-old. "You have to the count of three to do as I say, or I will kill your mother." Black smoke cascades out of Elise like a vile disease. Even Sunny's eyes bug out at her. "One!"

She must be stopped.

Electricity crackles through the air as Joy's volume rises. The reindeer join in singing "The Little Drummer Boy," and so do the elves around us.

They know. They understand the magnitude of what Christmas magic can do.

It is so much more powerful than black magic.

"Two!" Elise screeches.

"Ferret out the monsters," I whisper, planting Joy into the ground between my feet. Magic blasts through the snow like an ever-expanding wave made of blinding white light. Then it narrows into two straight beams.

One goes straight through my mother, widening her eyes and blowing her hair back before it barrels into Elise, exploding the elf into a rocket of fireworks and glitter. The second does the same to Sunny. If there had been any others in on this vile attempt on my father's life, my magic would have taken them out just as efficiently.

But there were only two traitors in our midst.

The knife Elise held drops harmlessly in front of Mom, sticking blade-down in the snow.

Gasps ring out over the courtyard, nearly drowning out the last note of the song resounding from Joy. I pull her from the ground and slip her back into her sheath. Silence blankets us.

And then my mother is on her feet, sprinting into Santa's arms. After a long, tight squeeze, she pulls away and begins frantically looking for the injuries that caused his coat to be soiled with blood. But she cannot find the source.

My father grabs her hands and tilts her chin up so she meets his gaze. "You will not find a scratch on me." He smiles down at her as his eyes sparkle with adoration.

"But how?" My mother waves at the obvious destruction of his suit.

He nods toward me. "Chrissy used Christmas magic to heal me."

"Me, too!" shouts Blitzen.

She turns to me, blinking madly as if her brain cannot comprehend the power of Christmas, even after the latest display. She rakes her eyes over my disheveled and torn coat, along with the patches covering my wounds on my arms and shoulder, but she does not leave my father's embrace.

I, unlike my father, am not healed. I offer her a smile and a shrug. "I might be in need of a doctor." I glance at the patches on my arm. Deep brownish-red spots show through the bandages.

"We will patch you up and then sit down for the feast," my mother says.

Her declaration seems to knock the elves back from the shock of seeing two of their own turn into glitter. They rush toward us as if they are welcoming us back from the dead.

"Um. About that. We might not want to trust the food that Elise made. It's probably tainted in some way," Santa says.

It only takes a moment before the entirety of the group groans at the prospect of not having a Christmas feast.

I glance around, and my gaze lands on the Winter Warlock. Even he looks troubled. He meets my gaze and steps forward.

"Perhaps I can help detect what may be tainted," he says almost sheepishly.

I smile at him, admonishing myself for even thinking this gentle giant of a man could ever have an evil bone in his body. "That would be nice."

"And then I can see what I can do for your wounds." He nods toward my soiled bandages.

I don't agree to that quite yet. I am more worried about poisoned food than a few drops of lost blood, so we lead him into the grand banquet room, where our tree reaches to the rafters and sparkles with lights and golden garland.

The banquet table stretches the entire length of the room with enough seating for the entire village. It's decorated in shades of red and green with gold and silver accents. A braid of evergreen stretches down the middle, illuminated by Christmas lights. Just like Santa's suit, it is a tradition and beautifully executed.

I suck in a breath and look at the serving tables. Dozens of dishes are laid out across them, with enough to feed us all for the next twelve days.

The Winter Warlock closes his eyes, and his hands move in smooth figure eights, creating a rainbow of sparkling magic. When he stretches his arms out, the colorful magic races to the buffet, leaping from dish to dish, swirling around them before jumping to the next.

Some dishes brighten and others turn to a pale gray mush as the magic touches them.

When his magic has touched all the dishes, it returns to him, filling his form with the rainbow spectrum before fading.

All the dishes Dad usually loads his plate with are all gray mush. Poisoned to make sure if we made it back alive, my father wouldn't survive the Christmas feast.

"Damn that elf," Santa says under his breath as he scans the table.

A quarter of the dishes need to go. With another push of the warlock's magic, the gray mush turns to smoke, disappearing from the tables altogether. The warlock's lips pull down into a deep frown as he shakes his head.

"They apparently did not care about collateral damage in their quest for power," he snaps, meeting my gaze. "Let's see what I can do for you."

"They didn't care about anyone but themselves." I look over what food remains, and my stomach roars to life. "My wounds can wait. My stomach can't."

We dig into what remains of the feast, loading our plates and taking a seat at the banquet table, trying to rekindle the true Christmas spirit.

And after we thank the Lord for the food before us as well as our safe return, the Winter Warlock asks, "Now tell us what in the Hades happened to you tonight."

Santa glances over at Mom and gently kisses her cheek before sending me a wink.

"It started off as a clear and silent night..." My father launches into the story of our harrowing Christmas Eve, with all the magic of a master storyteller.

The End

Thank you for reading SILENT NIGHT!

Continue Chrissy's story with
CHRISTMAS WISH.

# ABOUT J.E. TAYLOR

J.E. Taylor is a USA Today bestselling author, a publisher, an editor, a manuscript formatter, a mother, a wife, a business analyst, and a Supernatural fangirl, not necessarily in that order. She first sat down to seriously write in February of 2007 after her daughter asked:

"Mom, if you could do anything, what would you do?"

From that moment on, she hasn't looked back.

In addition to being co-owner of Novel Concept Publishing, Ms. Taylor also moonlights as a Senior Editor of Allegory E-zine, an online venue for Science Fiction, Fantasy and Horror, and co-hosts the popular YouTube talk show Spilling Ink.

She lives in New Hampshire with her husband and during the summer months enjoys her weekends on the shore in southern Maine.

Visit her at www.jetaylor75.com to check out all of her books.

# SILENT NIGHT TRILOGY

Most of the time, we deal with a stray rogue monster or two on Christmas Eve. But this year is different. It seems the monsters have decided they want to play with Santa's reindeer and ring his bells.

If I don't put a stop to this madness, not only will Santa be their next meal, but children all over the world will wake to a Christmas that never was.

If they wake at all...

Silent Night Trilogy includes Joy, Silent Night, and Christmas Wish.

You might also like these other urban fantasy and fantasy romance books by J.E. Taylor.

# SEASON OF THE DRAGON

**Monsters, trust issues, betrayal, and a near death experience.**

**What else could go wrong?**

The end of life as we knew it didn't come with a nuclear blast. It didn't come with the deadly impact of a hurdling asteroid. No. It came in a wave of illness that swept the world with fear, and in our quarantined silence, the monsters awoke.

Leviathans, serpent kings, and dragons came forth from the bowels of the Earth. The season of the dragon began with fire and fury and ended with a new world order. One in which these giant terrorists held all the power.

When Mikhail St. Clare betrays the monsters by saving me from death at their claws, I cannot trust the last remaining dragon shifter. Not when humankinds' survival is at stake, and he had a hand in our near extinction.

The only thing we seem to agree on is our desire to annihilate the leviathans and unseat the Serpent King. Our personal futures depend on ridding the earth of these murderous overlords.

We thought crossing the leviathan-patrolled city where every corner hides a hideous death was our most lethal hurdle. But building a bomb large enough to wipe out an entire species carries its own insane levels of danger.

One wrong move and we could destroy everyone living in New York instead.

# THE FALLEN VALKYRIE DUET

**A fallen Valkyrie. A Fae-Wraith hybrid.**

**Enemies become allies to survive a god's wrath.**

Odin's Order to reap an innocent soul from Earth makes me question everything I have ever known as a Valkyrie. Protecting the innocent is our basis for existing, and now I must decide. Do I blindly follow his order?

If I don't, I will be just another casualty in Odin and Thor's destruction of the realms. Anyone who challenges their rule dies a very public death, regardless of their origins. And now they have enslaved Earth.

Reyfyre, a fae-wraith hybrid, and one of Asgard's enemies, has been hiding in this realm his entire life. When he finds me, he offers asylum as long as I help him kill Odin and Thor.

With everything they have done, how can I refuse?

When a bounty is placed on my head, we make the decision to leave Reyfyre's mountain sanctuary and head to New York to get lost in the city of millions. But the trek across the Canadian wilderness brings us face to face with hidden refugees, predators, and thieves.

There's no other option but to survive.

If we die, then there will be no one left to stop the callous gods before they destroy the only realm left.

But are we strong enough to take down a god?

*If you like dark twists on Norse Mythology, you will love the Fallen Valkyrie duet.*

# RUNNING FROM THE DEVIL TRILOGY

**An escaped demon and a snarky cat face off against the seven deadly sins.**

Escaping from Hell was just the beginning of Phoebe's problems. In Hell, she had a position of legend. A marquis of torture. But on the human plane, she is just another New York City destitute.

Before she has a chance to get her bearings on the unforgiving streets, Fate steps in and offers her a chance at redemption, but it doesn't come cheap.

She must bring in the demons that escaped alongside her while making sure no humans are harmed in the process. In order to do that, she needs to learn to live in the human world with the help of another one of Fate's parolees, a snarky cat named Smoke.

If it means never seeing the halls of Hell again, Phoebe will do anything, even battle the seven deadly sins single-handed.

# FIRE CURSED TRILOGY

**Lucifer's daughter rises.**

Faith Kennedy's mother hid the awful truth from her daughter for sixteen years. Until she lay on her deathbed. Only then did she reveal who sired her daughter, and the revelation terrifies Faith.

The devil may have sired her, but he only wants her beating heart ripped out of her chest. After all, that's where her angel grace fueling her fire power is stored, and that will give him what he needs to bring about humanity's fall.

And Lucifer will take down anyone who gets in his way.

When Faith is given an ancient knife that can kill the devil, she faces the toughest challenge of her young life. She must hunt Lucifer and put him down. Otherwise, the world will burn.

But if she succeeds, she may wipe herself, and everyone she loves, out of existence.

This set includes Fire Cursed, Homecoming, and Judgement Day.

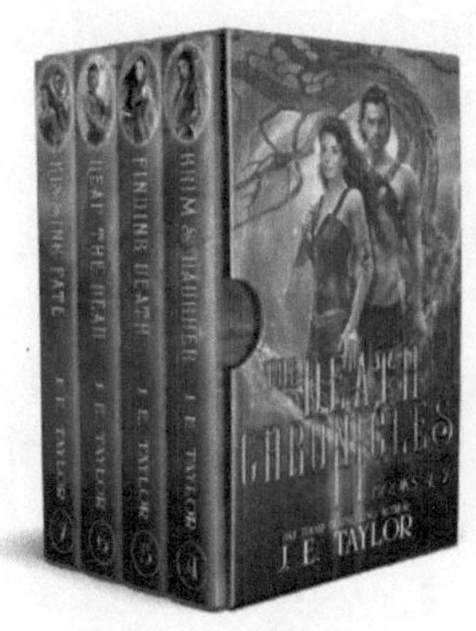

# THE DEATH CHRONICLES II

Death is the family business, but not one I want to pursue. Thankfully, it's been passed down from father to son for generations, so it should skip me as Death's daughter. Then I won't have to stop being alive and can actually live my life. Right?

Well, the reapers don't agree. And neither do the angels.

One thinks I'm destined to take over, the other believes I will destroy

existence. Both want me dead to match
their own agendas.

I have an agenda of my own, and
Leviathan who has sworn to protect
me. But once my family and friends
start being targeted, the family
business, while grim, might be the only
choice I have to save those I love.

The Death Chronicles *II* includes the
following titles

Grim's Daughter

Finding Death

Reap the Dead

Kissing Fate

# SHADES OF NIGHT

The Monster Defense Agency demands loyalty and prohibits inter-agency relationships. And once you become an agent, the only way out is in a body bag.

When Sarah Stone and Robby Young train together at the agency's academy, sparks fly. And when they are paired as partners, they must muzzle their attraction, or they will face a firing squad.

All their pent-up frustration sharpens them into finely tuned monster hunters. Their ability to neutralize entire nests of vampires becomes the stuff of legends.

But hunting vampires has its own risks. Especially when Sarah and Robby uncover duplicity and corruption at the highest echelon within the Monster Defense Agency.

With a bull's-eye on their backs from both the agency and the vampires they hunt, Sarah and Robby's only hope is to take down the Monster Defense Agency.

But two against an ancient organization that trains monster-killers and knows all their tricks is even harder than it sounds. It's going to take all their skill and intelligence to kill this beast.

And being caught is not an option.

Shades of Night delivers forbidden mates, cool magic, and a kick-ass heroine in this fast-paced urban fantasy series.

Books included in this special edition hardcover:

Young Blood – A Shades of Night Prequel

Wicked Heart – Shades of Night Book 1

Crooked Soul – Shades of Night Book 2

Tainted Mind – Shades of Night Book 3

# THE WITCH ASSASSIN

**An assassin tasked with taking out a mythical fae king...**

**In a realm that doesn't exist...**

Mya's mission is to get in, obtain the fae king's DNA, and get out.

It should be easy with her gifts, except when does anything ever go as planned?

But failing in her line of work is a death sentence, and nothing in her training prepared her for Tavin Zorander—the most powerful Elvren to ever exist.

After all, it's his family's magic that's kept his kingdom cloaked from the prying eyes of the universe for centuries.

When she finds herself at the mercy of the fae king, Mya has a choice to make.

Does she use her darkest power, thus compromising her mission, or should she surrender to Tavin's desires and put his entire kingdom at risk?

# A FRACTURED FAIRY TALE

# BOOKS 1-10

Little Red Riding Hood, Cinderella, Brave, Rapunzel, Frozen, Snow White, Sleeping Beauty, Aladdin, Beauty and the Beast and Peter Pan – all fairy tales you know and love, but twisted, fractured into something new.

Shifters and magic claw through the pages of these fractured fairy tales, giving you a thrilling take on an old tale.

Will the heroine survive whatever the evil villain has in store?  Or will Love conquer all?

Grab your hard cover copy of A Fractured Fairy Tale – books 1-10 and find out!

A Fractured Fairy Tale books 1-10 includes

Red, Cinder, Brave, Tangled, Frozen, Snow, Spindle, Jasmine, Belle, Hook

Find these titles and other fantasy and
suspense titles on J.E. Taylor's website!

www.JETaylor75.com